FAMILY TIES

JONATHAN DUNSKY

1

I heard the rumble of the sports car's engine a moment before the knock on the door. It was my cousin Jimmy, with a hangdog look on his bulldog face. Jimmy's refrigerator shoulders were encased in a tight leather jacket. His sledgehammer hands hung at his sides, car keys jutting from one massive fist. Even though he stood on the second of three steps to my trailer home, he looked down at me. Jimmy had always been big, and in the two and a half years since we last saw each other, he'd only gotten bigger across the shoulders and chest.

"Hey, Mike," Jimmy said, his voice as deep as his barrel chest. Despite the chill of the night, Jimmy's black scalp was beaded with sweat. His deep-set eyes had fear in them. I got a sick feeling in my stomach. Jimmy was about to drag me into something nasty again.

"Hey, Jimmy." We clasped hands, and he pulled me into a bear hug. I was surprised to realize I had missed him. Even after all I'd been through, and his part in it, I had missed him.

I moved back to let him enter. The trailer sagged under his weight. I waved my hand around and said, "Welcome. It's not much, but it beats a jail cell."

This was true on both counts. The trailer was better and bigger than my jail cell had been, but it wasn't much. There was one long and narrow space. On one end was a small niche with a bed, on the other a tiny kitchenette. In the middle was the living area, with a secondhand couch, a scarred wooden coffee table, a fifteen-inch TV, and two plastic folding chairs. There was a pizza box on the table, a bottle of beer beside it.

I was embarrassed that Jimmy was seeing this. I used to have cars, a big apartment, more women than I could handle. All the things that ill-gotten money could buy. Jimmy still had those things. Because Jimmy never went to jail for the crimes we'd committed. I had. And now that I was out and working the only kind of honest job an ex-con could get—a minimum wage one—I could no longer afford the things Jimmy still could.

I got an extra beer from the mini-fridge, and Jimmy helped himself to some pizza.

"This is nice," Jimmy said. "Real nice."

I could always tell when Jimmy was lying. He wouldn't be caught dead living in this dump. From the sound of its engine, his car had cost more than I would make in three years packing groceries, maybe even longer.

"Sorry I didn't come visit you sooner," Jimmy said.

I told him not to worry about it. The truth was, I wanted him to stay away. Don't get me wrong, I loved him, always have and always will, but I needed time to settle in. I also did a lot of thinking while I was locked up. I knew that Jimmy was bad news. He was deep in the life and would never turn straight. And I wanted to turn straight. I wanted never to be in a cage again.

Jimmy finished his slice of pizza and wiped sauce from his fingers.

"I need some help," he said.

"If this is about a job, Jimmy, then no. I'm out of the life. I've seen the consequences, and they aren't pretty. They're so bad this trailer looks like the Taj Mahal to me."

Jimmy frowned, and I realized that my cousin didn't know what the Taj Mahal was. He didn't ask, though, so I didn't say anything.

"It's not about a job. I'm in serious trouble, and I got no one else who will help me."

2

The trouble was lying across the backseat of Jimmy's Jag. She was young and white and dressed for misadventure. Her red dress was short to begin with, but the way her legs were curled made the hem ride indecently high on her thighs. One of her arms dangled over the seat, her bright-red fingernails brushing the floor mat. Her eyes were half open and drool was coming out of her mouth.

I didn't want to touch her, didn't want to be anywhere near her. But there she was, way too young, way too sexy for her age. And way too still to be good news.

"Christ, Jimmy. What happened?"

I heard the creak of the leather jacket as Jimmy shrugged.

"We were having a bit of fun, is all. Fooled around, drank a bit, and I had some dope on me, and—"

I turned to face him. "What kind of dope?"

"Heroin."

"You gave this girl heroin? How old is she, fifteen?"

"Seventeen. What difference does it make? How do I wake her up?"

I touched the girl on the neck. She was cold. It took me a

moment to find her pulse. It was erratic, fast one moment, slow the next. Like her heart couldn't make up its mind whether to keep on beating or not.

"She needs a doctor. We need to take her to a hospital."

Jimmy was shaking his head before I finished my sentence.

"No way. I can't take her to no hospital."

"We can drop her off at the entrance to the emergency room," I said, thinking, What is this we stuff? How did this get to be my problem?

"No, man. That ain't good. What if someone sees us? I ain't going to jail for this."

"She could die, Jimmy."

"What about that guy who once mended you when you got that bullet in your leg?"

"Doc Gomez? That was four years ago, and he was a drunk even then."

"But you know where he lives, right?"

I looked at Jimmy and saw that he would not be swayed. He wouldn't be taking this girl to a hospital, no matter how bad of a shape she was in. I shook my head, taking a deep breath.

"You got cash on you?" I asked.

"Sure."

"How much? We'll need a grand, at least."

Jimmy had eight hundred dollars and change on him. I cursed and ran into my trailer. I had almost five hundred dollars that I'd squirreled away over the past few months since I'd been out. I'd been eating poorly and meagerly to save that money. I yanked the blanket off my bed, ran to the car, and covered the unconscious girl with it.

"Get in," I said to Jimmy. "Drive."

3

Doc Gomez lived in a run-down tenement building in a part of town where streetlights had a lifespan of less than two weeks and potholes went untended for years.

The streets were nearly deserted at that time of night and there was ample parking. Jimmy parked the car and said, "This better be quick. We take too long, the car may not be here when we get back."

I got out of the car. "C'mon. I need your help with her. I can't carry her up four flights of stairs."

It turned out that Jimmy could. The girl looked like a child in his massive arms, her legs dangling over one arm, her head over the other. If Jimmy was making an effort, he was doing a good job of hiding it.

The stairway was dark and dank. It stank of spilled beer, cooked meat, and cigarette smoke, so I made sure to breathe through my mouth all the way up. Fortunately, the lights in the second and third landings still worked. I climbed quickly, followed by Jimmy's heavy footsteps.

On the fourth floor were two doors. I knocked on the one

marked 7. The first few knocks went unanswered, so I knocked harder, hollering, "Open up, Doc! This is urgent business."

I put my ear to the door and heard shuffling steps. Two seconds later a bolt was slid back and the door opened. Doc Gomez stood on the threshold, barefooted, wearing a tattered pair of tan sweatpants and a stained Yankees T-shirt. White whiskers covered his sunken cheeks and his horn-rimmed eyeglasses were smudged. His hair was gray and thinning, his ears large and protruding. An unlit cigarette dangled from the corner of his mouth. He held a soda bottle in his left hand.

"You pound on the door any harder, the building will collapse around it," Doc said. If he'd seen the girl in Jimmy's arms, his face didn't register it.

"I was worried you were sleeping," I said.

"Men my age never sleep. It's a medical fact. Well, not really, but it's the closest thing to it. If I were drinking, now, that would be a different story. Some scotch or vodka in me, and I'd sleep like the dead. But I'm not drinking these days. Trying to turn a new leaf." Doc Gomez burst out laughing. He had a smoker's laugh, like crunched glass being stepped on. He coughed once, and his cigarette dropped to the floor. He started bending for it, but his movements were shaky, and it was clear they caused him some pain.

I bent down and got the cigarette. I handed it to Doc. "We need your help, Doc."

Doc nodded sadly. "So I see. Cradle snatching, huh? Bring her in. You got money? I'm not running a charity here."

Doc led us down a carpeted hall. There was dust on every surface, a couple of dead cockroaches with their feet sticking up like antennae in the corners. We went past a living room, where a ratty recliner stood facing a TV that was quietly playing a Spanish news program. A scatter of empty Coke bottles surrounded the recliner. We got to a small room where an old medical examination bed stood. The room was a stark contrast to the rest of the place. It was pristine, every surface gleaming. A diploma hung proudly on the wall above the examination bed, proclaiming that Doc Gomez had graduated Harvard Medical School. His fall had been long and hard, but he was still good at his job. When he wasn't wasted.

I told him about the heroin, and Doc just shook his head. He told Jimmy to set the girl on the bed. He took a swig from the soda bottle and handed it to me. "Hold this for me, will ya?"

Doc checked the girl's pulse, then looked into her eyes. There was a cabinet behind him and he opened one of its drawers. Neat rows of labeled bottles stood within, and Doc picked one and filled a syringe with ocher fluid. "It will cost you fifteen hundred."

I showed him the money we had, and he settled for it with a grunt. With practiced movements he plunged the needle into the vein at the crook of the girl's arm.

He checked her pulse again, giving a nod that I interpreted as satisfactory. Then he ran his hands over the girl, first her legs, and then her arms, belly, breasts. One hand slipped under her skirt, massaging her thigh. I suddenly recalled the rumors about why Doc had lost his license. Something to do with underage patients. I could feel Jimmy's eyes on me. He sensed something was wrong here.

"Doc," I said in a sharp voice, "let's keep this professional."

Doc Gomez turned his eyes on me. There was something in them. A dirty sort of hunger and anger that I had interrupted him. But his hands stopped roaming over the girl. "If you wanted a professional, why come here? I am, after all, not a professional anymore. I can work better than most of them, in their fancy white coats, in their fancy clinics, but I am no longer a professional." He returned his gaze to the girl, sighed a longing sigh that made my skin crawl, and said, "It's good that you didn't wait longer."

4

Doc put the empty syringe aside. His eyes were fastened on the girl. I saw that her breathing was becoming deeper and a little color had returned to her cheeks.

"She'll be out for a while longer," Doc said. "She'll wake up thirsty as hell. Hungry too. Give her whatever she asks for."

Doc reached a liver-spotted hand to brush the girl's hair away from her eyes. I was ready to stop him if he went any further, but Doc's hand paused midair above the girl's exposed face. He frowned, then took hold of her chin and turned her face so it was angled toward him.

When he turned to me, his face was white. "You want to get me killed, bringing me this girl? You crazy?"

"What are you talking about, Doc?" From the corner of my eye I saw Jimmy straighten from his slouch against the wall.

"You fuckhead," Doc said. "You stupid, stupid punk. You're telling me you don't even know who she is?"

Spittle was flying from Doc's mouth now, and he jabbed a finger at my chest.

I was shaking my head, wondering what came over him, when Jimmy entered my peripheral vision. Actually, it was his

.45 that came into view first. I was starting to turn when the gun fired. The bang slapped my ears like a whip. The cramped room amplified the blast of the gun, echoing from wall to wall. Doc's head was thrown back, a spray of red gushing out the back of it, splashing the wall behind him. Doc's body crashed into the wall and slid to the floor, trailing blood and brain matter behind it. The girl didn't even move.

I screamed and grabbed Jimmy's hand. I tried tearing the gun away, but his grip was like an iron vise. Not that it would have mattered. Doc had died before he hit the wall.

"Are you nuts? Why'd you shoot him?"

Jimmy lowered his gun. His face was impassive. "He recognized her. He might've talked."

It took me a moment to remember the girl. Doc had been terrified by her.

"Who is she, Jimmy?"

"Carlota Zamprini."

The name was like a physical blow. I shut my eyes, feeling my chest constrict around my heart. It was hard to get oxygen in all of a sudden, so I gulped for air. The smell of gunpowder and blood got in my nostrils and mouth, and I nearly gagged.

"Zamprini. As in Pablo Zamprini?"

"His daughter."

We're dead, I thought. *I'm dead and so is Jimmy.* All because he went and doped up the daughter of a main boss. Pablo Zamprini would have both our heads. Jimmy had dragged me down again, only this time the outcome wouldn't be a two-year stint in jail. This time I would end up shot by Zamprini's men. In fact, I would be lucky if they shot me. At least that would be quick.

"Goddammit, Jimmy. You got no self-control. First, you go out with Zamprini's daughter and pump her full of dope. Then, you end up shooting Doc Gomez."

"He knew who she was," Jimmy said in a petulant voice. "He would have blabbed."

"Think, Jimmy. Think. Why would he do that? He's part of it now, the moment he let us in the door. That was why he got so upset just before you put a fucking bullet in his head."

I ran a hand over my face. My palm was cold and I was sweating, and my heart was tap-dancing against my breastbone. We had to get out of there. We needed to clean up whatever we could and then we had to get out of there. No one knew we had come to Doc Gomez, and in this neighborhood, no one would call the cops just because someone fired a gun.

Then the girl whimpered in her doped-up sleep.

"Grab the girl and go back to the car," I said. "I'll come right down."

5

I wiped every surface I could think of, anywhere either of us might have touched. Carefully, so as not to get any blood on me, I retrieved our money from Doc's pocket. I exited the apartment, forcing myself to walk down at a regular pace. Jimmy was already in the car, engine idling. I got in and said, "Go, go."

Jimmy pulled away from the curb. "Where we headed?"

"Just drive. I need to think."

I turned to the window, watching tenements blur by. I thought about how this was a familiar scene. How Jimmy had always gotten me into trouble, ever since we were kids. Like how we were caught stealing sodas from a neighborhood kiosk. Like how I went to jail for the robbery we committed, while Jimmy remained free. And now this. Now my life was in danger. I could let Jimmy handle things himself. No one knew I was involved. The girl was still out and Doc was dead. But I couldn't do that. Jimmy was family. He and his mother had taken me in after my mother died. Jimmy's mother had raised me, and when she was dying from cancer, she made me promise to always look out for Jimmy. I was the coolheaded one, while Jimmy was unpredictable. Jimmy could get into trouble because he had no self-control and didn't think things through. He was stupid enough to give dope to Pablo Zamprini's jailbait girl. He wasn't smart enough to think of a solution. It was up to me to figure out a way out of this.

Jimmy said, "I could do her, you know."

"Huh?"

"The girl. I could take care of her."

It took me three seconds to catch on. "You're not going to kill her, Jimmy."

"But—"

"You're not killing her! Damn it, if you were going to pop her, you should have done it before you came to me. It would have been dumb as hell even then, but at least I'd be out of it."

"I'm sorry, man. Didn't mean to get you in trouble. I just didn't know where to turn."

"It's alright," I lied.

"And it's not like I want to kill Carlota. She's a sweet kid. We had fun together."

"Okay, Jimmy."

"But maybe it's the only way now."

I turned to Jimmy and through gritted teeth said, "If we kill her, we'd be dead men walking. There'd be no coming back from this. Right now, while she's still alive, there may still be a way to get out of it. If we kill her, if she dies, no matter how, it's over. Her father will not rest until we're dead. Got it?"

Jimmy nodded. "So what do we do?"

"I need to think," I said. "Let me think for a while, okay? Just drive."

Twenty minutes later I had a plan. It was sordid and it made me sick to my stomach, but it just might work. And we had nothing to lose.

6

It didn't take much to get Jimmy to go along. He actually chuckled when I told him the plan, said I had a sick mind. What could I say? Fuck you, Jimmy, for putting me in this position that I have to do this? It wouldn't help none.

The girl came to shortly after we were done. She blinked her eyes several times, orienting herself. Jimmy was outside, smoking or getting off, or both, so I watched her as she opened her eyes in my narrow bed in my scummy trailer. She sat up straight when she saw me, her eyes big fearful ovals.

I handed her a bottle of water. "Here."

She snatched the bottle from my hand, then scooted back as far as she could. I moved back a step, giving her more space. She gulped down the water. Some of it ran down her throat.

She eyed me suspiciously, clutching the empty bottle as if it were a weapon. I noted how small she was. She seemed even younger now that she was awake, and I cursed Jimmy for what we'd done to her.

"What happened?" she asked. Her voice was small and soft. "Where am I?"

"You overdosed," I said. "You were out for a while. But you're going to be fine."

She looked at me, and I realized I hadn't answered her second question.

"You're at my place. It's a trailer. Soon you'll be going home."

"Who are you? What's your name?"

"I'm Mike. Jimmy's cousin."

Her eyes narrowed. "Jimmy? Jimmy's a part of this?"

A part of what? I thought, and realized that the answer had become too complicated, too crazy.

"I want to go home," she said.

"Soon."

"I want to go home right now." She was nearly shouting now. "Do you know who my father is?"

"Soon," I said. "I promise."

Jimmy came back, attracted by her raised voice.

"Everything all right in here?" he asked.

"Damn you, Jimmy," the girl said. "What's going on? This little asshole won't tell me anything."

"Stay with her," I told him. "I need to make some calls."

I stepped outside. I breathed in the scent of the early dawn, glad to be away from the girl. Away from my recent sin.

7

It was noon when I met Mr. Fry in a coffee shop. He was the right-hand man of old man Zamprini. He handled delicate, personal, as well as business matters. He was working on a slice of cheesecake when I arrived. He had taken the booth farthest from the door. Two booths closer to the entrance, a pair of solid-looking men with stony expressions were watching every step I took from the door to Mr. Fry's booth.

I sat. Mr. Fry put down his fork and smiled at me. The smile didn't touch his eyes. Mr. Fry—I didn't know his first name—had straight teeth and deep dimples. His smile would look charming to anyone who didn't know what he did for a living. I did know, so his smile brought to mind a shark. He had blue eyes and sandy hair. He was tall and lean and had a mild, healthy-looking tan. His suit was navy with subdued stripes. The suit had probably cost more than I made in a month. No, make that three months. His burgundy tie looked like a one-month paycheck. I was glad I couldn't see his shoes.

"The cake here is good," Mr. Fry said. "Want some?"

I noticed that he made sure to finish his bite before speaking. He was cultured, meticulous, well mannered. When he laced his fingers on the tabletop, I saw that his nails had been manicured. He had a signet ring on one pinkie, silver with a red stone.

"Not hungry," I said. "Thanks for meeting me in person."

He waved a hand. "This is urgent business. Family business. We need to get this thing over with quickly. Where's the girl?"

"She's safe."

"And where's your cousin?"

"He's with her."

Mr. Fry's smooth forehead wrinkled in a frown. "I don't understand."

I took a steadying breath. "I want to make sure Jimmy will not be hurt once you get the girl back."

Mr. Fry's frown deepened; then he started to laugh. "I was told you went to jail for your cousin, that you were loyal, but I didn't believe it. Money trumps everything, I said. He's going to sell him out. Besides, once word gets out about your cousin, once we go after him, you may be caught in the crossfire. You're smart, you know that. But you're actually trying to save his life despite the risk it puts you in." Mr. Fry leaned forward and his tone turned hard. "Listen to me, you moron. This is not the time to play games. I want the girl and I want her right now. What happens to your cousin is out of my hands. He was dumb enough to take Carlota out, and he will pay the price. Old man Zamprini doesn't like anyone messing with his daughter. Especially—" Mr. Fry's mouth twitched in distaste, "—niggers—as he puts it. His words, not mine."

Mr. Fry looked out the coffee shop's window before turning back to me. "Here I was, ready to pay you handsomely for your cousin, but you don't want money, do you?"

I shook my head.

Mr. Fry sighed. His voice was as sharp as a steak knife. "You either tell us where he and the girl are, or today will be your last dose of sunshine. You'll be escorted out, pushed into a car, taken somewhere dark. Someone will be waiting for you there. Someone who knows pain and likes to administer it. You will tell us everything. You can count on it."

His eyes were like blue ice, and my knees started to shake, rattling the tabletop. It was now or never. Soon, I wouldn't have any nerve left. I fished the envelope of photos from my pocket and slid it across the table to him.

His eyes twitched down, puzzled. He picked up the envelope, took out the photos, and his eyes grew wide. He flicked through them, his jaw clenching tighter with each picture till I thought his teeth might snap. There were ten in total, each more depraved and degrading than the next. He paused at the photo of Jimmy sticking his cock in the sleeping girl's mouth. The other pictures were of a similar vein. They weren't quality pictures—we'd taken them with Jimmy's phone and the lighting was bad—but they were clear enough to make out her face.

He held up one picture. A naked Carlota was in bed with a naked Jimmy beside her. Her body was completely bare. Jimmy was cupping one of her breasts, grinning like an idiot. I had a sick feeling just looking at the photo, and it was only half of what I had felt taking it.

"What the hell is this?" Mr. Fry said in a voice thick with rage.

I made myself give him a direct, flat stare. "It's a deal offer. You let Jimmy and me live, no reprisals, no payback, and these pictures stay private. And you get Carlota back, of course." I paused for a moment. "Her safety is not up for negotiation in any way, Mr. Fry. I won't let anything happen to her."

"Except ruin her name, you mean." He took a deep breath. "You have gigantic balls, I give you that. A tiny brain, but gigantic balls. You're being an idiot. You see that, don't you? You'd be branded for life."

I'm already branded, I thought. *I'm an ex-con who's gone straight. I've got the mark of Cain on me already.*

"If these pictures go public, your boss will lose face. He'll be seen as a joke. People will say he can't control his own daughter, having her be a whore for niggers—your words, not mine. They'll wonder whether he could handle his business any better."

Mr. Fry was silent for a moment. Then he said, "Your cousin isn't worth this. He's trash."

"He is not trash!" I spat out, and felt a wicked sort of satisfaction at seeing Mr. Fry blink. "He is family and I'm sticking by him. If anything happens to him, the pictures go public. If anything happens to me, the pictures go public. I've set it up so it's automatic. Computers work that way. Even an uneducated ghetto kid like me knows enough technology to do that. You may try to beat it out of me, but I bet I can last long enough so the pictures will go out anyway. Do we have a deal?"

I could see his mind working. He was running options in his mind, trying to see whether he could trap me somehow. I hoped I was right and that he couldn't.

A silent moment later, he said, "Fine. It's a deal."

I left him the pictures. I could always print more.

8

I exited the coffee shop and called Jimmy to let him know that it was fine to leave the girl in the Ford Focus he had stolen earlier that day. I called Mr. Fry and told him the corner where the car was parked. He hung up without saying anything.
"Let's go," I said to Jimmy. "You can drive me back."
Jimmy got a cigarette going as he drove, and I rolled down the window to let the smoke out. We didn't talk much on the way to the trailer park. Jimmy tried a couple of times, talking about mundane stuff like basketball and some girl he was seeing. Nothing that happened the previous night, not Doc's murder nor the girl's degradation, had any effect on him. He suddenly seemed like a stranger to me. He was still family, and I still loved him, but I didn't like him no more. I was tired, both of him and from lack of sleep.
"Listen, Jimmy," I said as he pulled up next to my trailer. "I think it'd be good if we didn't see each other any time soon. I need to stay clean. I can't have no more nights like this."
Jimmy took a deep breath, his shoulders moving up like a cresting wave. "If that's the way you want it, Mike. But I just want to say that I appreciate what you did."

"Don't see that girl again," I said.

He laughed, and in that laugh was the Jimmy I loved. That Jimmy wasn't so quick with a gun or indifferent to the honor of women. I wondered whether I would have done what I did for the Jimmy I saw last night, regardless of family ties and promises I'd made.

I got out of the car, told him to take care, and headed into my trailer. I was worn all over, my limbs leaded, my eyes stinging. I took off my clothes and crashed into bed. I was out in ten seconds.

9

They found Jimmy in his car. Someone had waited for him in the backseat and put two nine-millimeter rounds in his back. Shot him right through the front seat. Then he put one in his head, just to make certain.

The story made page four of the paper five days after we delivered Carlota to Mr. Fry. It was during work, while I was packing grocery bags for suburban wives, that I saw it. It wasn't the report on Jimmy's execution that caught my eye, though. It was the bigger story splashed across the front page, the one detailing the death of Pablo Zamprini, kingpin, mega-criminal, head mobster. When I saw it, I dropped the container of milk I'd been holding, picked up the newspaper, and scanned through it.

Zamprini was found in his office, revolver in hand, a bullet in his skull. There was speculation whether it was a suicide or a forced change of power at the highest level of local organized crime. The report continued on page four, and it was there, in a small box at the bottom of the page, that I learned about Jimmy.

For a moment the world around me ceased to exist. I was in a cocoon of silence and loss. It wasn't until the day manager, Mr. Cronin, kept calling me that I snapped out of it and started packing groceries again. Two minutes later, I left the store through the back exit and ran for the bus that would take me back to my trailer.

I was throwing clothes into a knapsack when I heard the car. I peeked out a window and saw a black Mercedes with tinted windows. Two beefy guys got out of the front seat. I recognized them. They'd been at the coffee shop where I'd met Mr. Fry.

I didn't have a gun. I was halfway to the kitchen and the knife drawer when the door was thrown open. The two guys came in. One of them drew the lapel of his jacket aside and I saw the butt of an automatic in a shoulder holster. The other motioned for me to go outside.

"In the car," he said. "Come on."

One of the goons held the back door of the car open for me. I looked at him, puzzled. This didn't feel like a hit. He said nothing, so I slid into the spacious seat, and he shut the door behind me.

Mr. Fry was seated inside. He was impeccably dressed in a dark-blue suit over a white dress shirt and a blood-red tie. He gave me an amiable smirk. His hands were folded in his lap. This time I noticed his shoes—black wingtips, polished bright.

He handed me a thick envelope. "Here."

I took it. Inside was a stack of bills, thick as a gun magazine, loose and crisp. Benjamin Franklin's face peered at me from each bill. I raised an eyebrow.

"Ten thousand dollars," Mr. Fry said. "Just in case you were wondering."

"What's it for?"

Mr. Fry's smile deepened. "One envelope for the one you gave me. The one with all those delicious and explosive pictures."

I must have looked puzzled as hell because he erupted in laughter, the scent of expensive scotch on his breath.

"Haven't you read the paper? Zamprini is gone, dead, burning in Hell as we speak. There's a new king in town."

His smile seemed to strain at the seams of his face with the immensity of his satisfaction.

"You?" I said, though there was no real question here.

"Yes. I'm no longer the adviser, no mere counselor. I took those pictures that you gave me and showed them to Zamprini. You're not the only one to whom family is paramount. He was quite willing to do anything I asked in order to spare his daughter the embarrassment of having those pictures made public." He paused for a moment, then said, "He was getting older, you know. And sick. When he was younger, I wouldn't have had the guts to do it. But I knew how much he loved Carlota. She was born when he was over fifty, and she made him soft." His eyes found mine. "But those pictures were the way to break him. Better than any overt mutiny. He simply handed the whole thing over. Just to keep her reputation. Family often makes us do stupid, illogical things."

I looked down at the money in my hand and back up at him.

"Does this mean I don't have to look over my shoulder for the rest of my life?"

His smile disappeared and he gave me a steady stare. "As long as you keep your mouth shut. No one knows you were involved, and I don't want anyone to know. Just as long as you keep quiet and get out of town, out of the state. Truth is, I like you, and without you I couldn't have done this. I don't want to kill you."

He gave me a friendly pat on my knee, smiling again.

I should have taken the money and got out of the car then, but family makes us do stupid, illogical things. So I asked, "And Jimmy?"

"That wasn't me," he said. "That was Zamprini's last order. It's too bad that you could see your cousin's face in those pictures.

Otherwise, he wouldn't have had to die. But there was no other way. You see that, right?"

I wasn't seeing much of anything. My mouth was dry and I heard my heart hammering in my ears. Those pictures, the ones I'd made to protect Jimmy, got him killed surer than if I'd done nothing. At least then he would have been on his guard.

"Mike? Mike, are you with me?" Mr. Fry's voice was louder than before, and I sensed he'd said my name a few times with no reaction from me. I turned to him. "You alright?" he asked. "I need to go. I want you out of town by tonight."

I nodded and got out of the car. His man closed the door, got into the front passenger seat, and they drove off.

I stood in the sun-drenched parking lot, sweat building under my shirt. I looked at the money and then at the tail of the receding Mercedes. I wondered what sort of guns and ammo I could buy with ten thousand dollars, and whether they would be enough to go after Mr. Fry.

"Fucking hell, Jimmy," I muttered. "Here you go dragging me down after you again."

AFTERWORD

Dear reader,

I want to thank you for reading my story. Stories are written to be shared, and you've done me a great honor by journeying with me through this tale.

If you enjoyed *Family Ties*, I would appreciate it if you would take the time to write a review on whatever website you use to purchase or review books.

I also invite you to check out my historical mystery series featuring private detective Adam Lapid. The first book in the series in *Ten Years Gone*.

I would also love to hear from you. Write me at contact@jonathandunsky.com with any questions or feedback.

ABOUT THE AUTHOR

Jonathan Dunsky lives in Israel with his wife and two sons. He enjoys reading, writing, and goofing around with his kids. He is the author of the Adam Lapid Mysteries series and the standalone thriller The Payback Girl.

COPYRIGHT INFORMATION

Family Ties
Jonathan Dunsky
Copyright © 2016 by Jonathan Dunsky
Cover by Vicovers
Cover art © defotoberg / depositphotos.com

All rights reserved. No part of this book may be used, reproduced or transmitted in any form or by any means, electronic or mechanical, including photocopying, recording, or by any information storage or retrieval system, without the written permission of the publisher, except where permitted by law, or in the case of brief quotations embodied in critical articles and reviews. For information, contact contact@jonathandunsky.com

Thank you for respecting the hard work of this author.

This is a work of fiction. Names, characters, places and incidents either are the creation of the author's imagination or are used fictitiously, and any resemblance to actual persons living or dead, business establishments, events or locales is entirely coincidental.

Visit JonathanDunsky.com for news and information.

Printed in Great Britain
by Amazon